To Musettes and carvers, One and all . . .
    Mekeel McBride in particular.
            — R.A.

For Greta and all who love her,
especially my Anderson family.
            — S.A.

Text copyright © 2003 Rick Agran
Adapted from the poem "Shivaree"
    published in CROW MILK
    (Oyster River Press, 1997)
        Illustrations
copyright © 2003 Sara Anderson
    Design collaboration:
Allison Kay & Sara Anderson
    All rights reserved
    CIP Data is available

Published in the United States in 2003
        by Handprint Books
        413 Sixth Avenue
    Brooklyn, New York 11215
    www.handprintbooks.com
        First Edition
        Printed in China
    ISBN: 1-59354-006-X

2 4 6 8 10 9 7 5 3 1

Pumpkin Shivaree

by Rick Agran

illustrated by Sara Anderson

Handprint Books
Brooklyn, New York

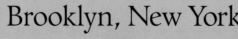

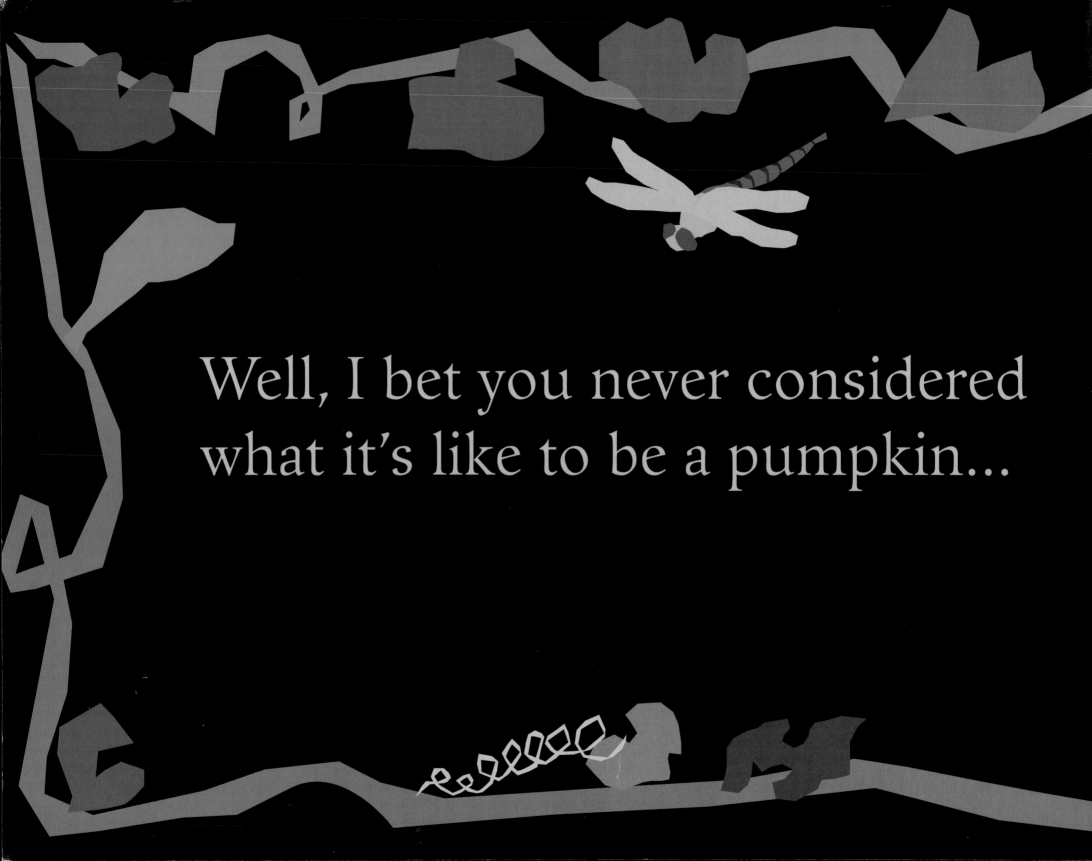

Well, I bet you never considered what it's like to be a pumpkin...

Across the pumpkin field
to the edge of the pasture
long green vines wander and twine.

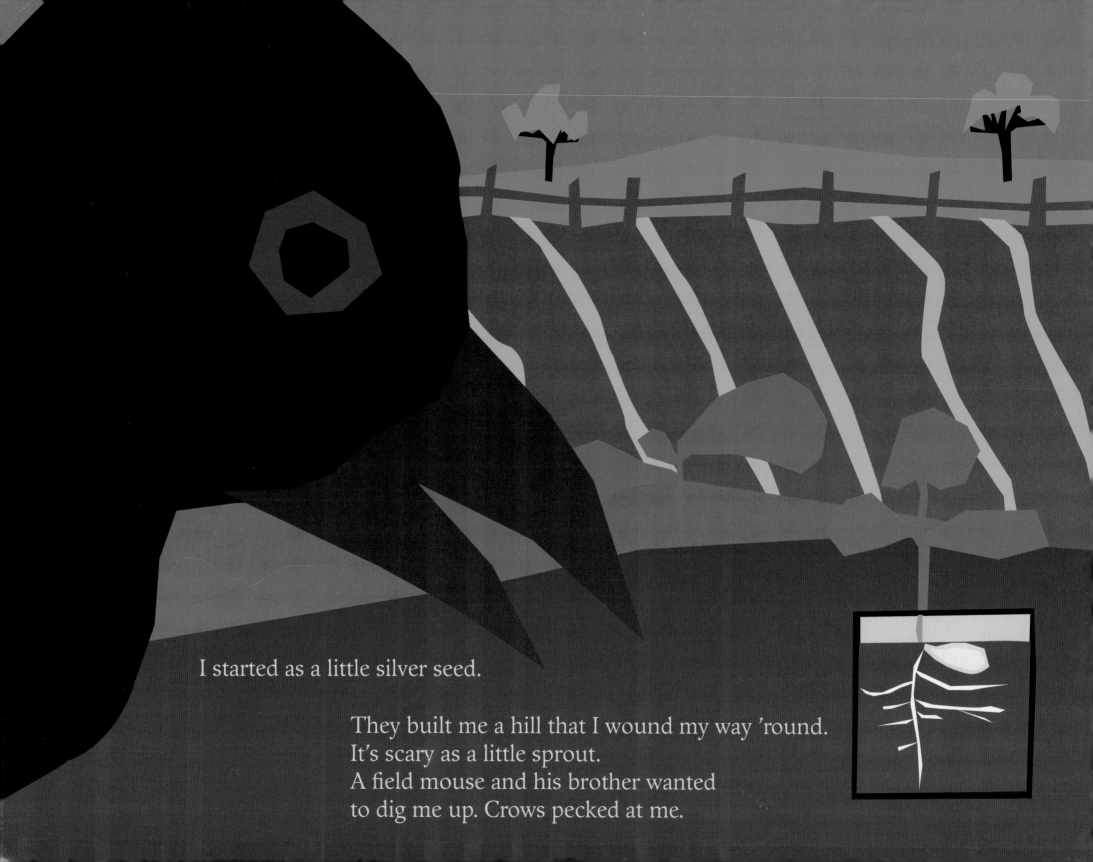

I started as a little silver seed.

They built me a hill that I wound my way 'round.
It's scary as a little sprout.
A field mouse and his brother wanted
to dig me up. Crows pecked at me.

When an aphid nibbled,
an ant came and kicked her off.
An inchworm tried to measure me,
but I was still too small.

Spring rain clouds almost drown me. A growing vine
lifted me out of the mud. I hid under deep green leaves
when sun tried to wrinkle me. A girl, humming
and weeding, almost stepped on me.

"Why do you hide in the shade, little blossom?
Come out in the sun. I want you to grow."

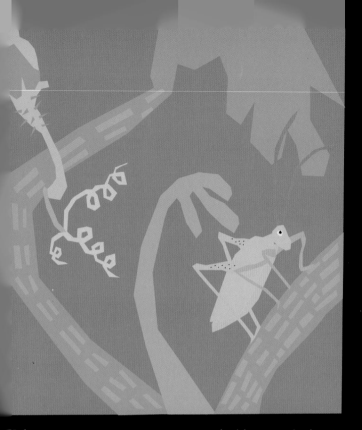
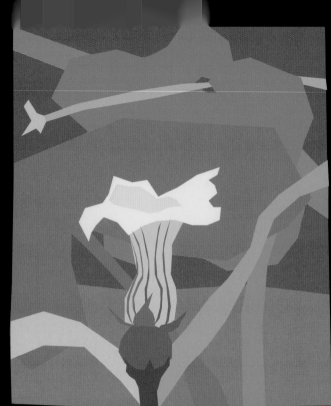

Shoots sprout. Tendrils twirl. Leaves unfold green shade. Bugs and bees pollinate. Pistil and stamen

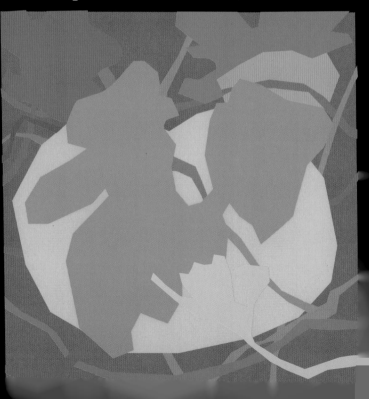

Flower then fruit. Tickle of six little feet. Savor rain. Drink sun. Grow toward a glow. Round and ripen.

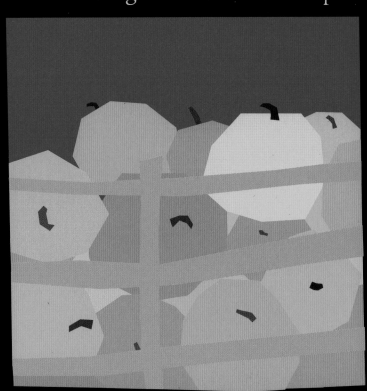

Talk of fall frostbite, a season of picking, plucking and carving.
Pumpkin smashing and Thanksgiving mashing.

They'll bake us and moosh us for pies or roast our insides.
No wonder we hide!

Brrrrr! It's frosty this morning. I'm picked with a slice, twist and tug. I'm tucked in the crook of her arm. Across the field and pasture with her, excited and scared, I've never been anywhere . . .

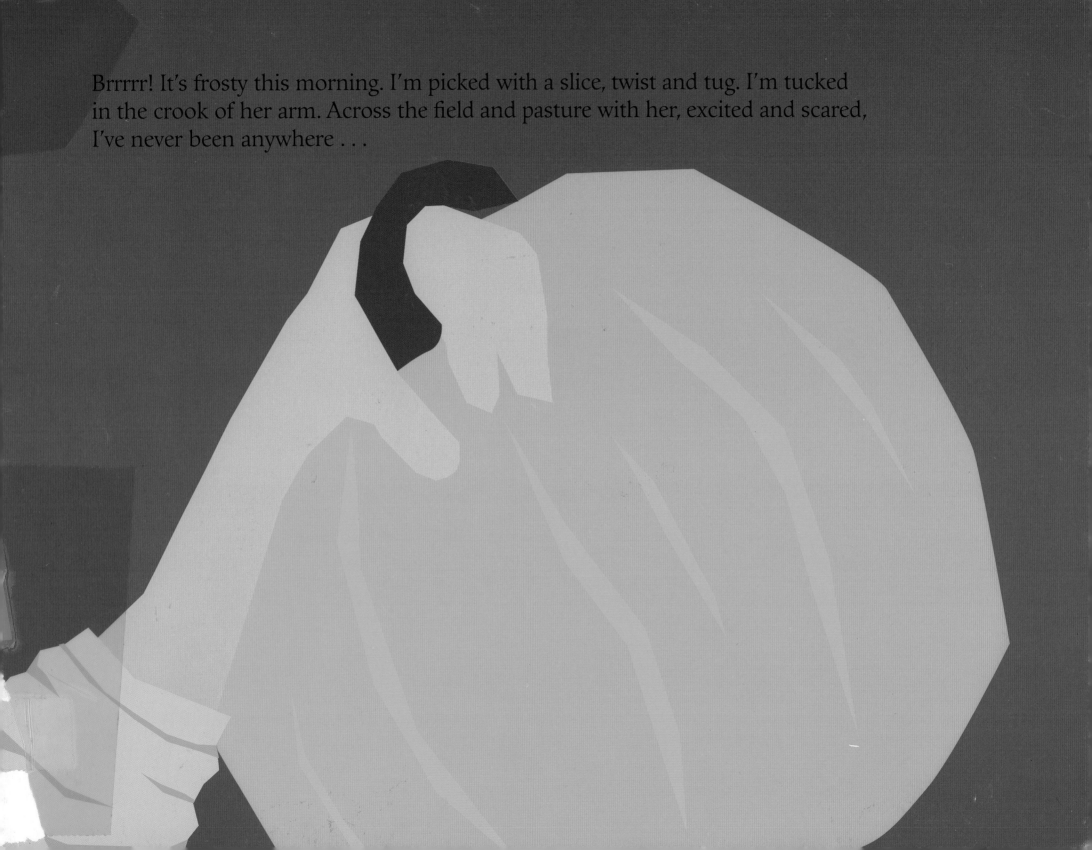

On the porch
she thumps my belly
like a baby drum.
She plunks me down
on old newspaper.

She opens her jack-o'-lantern knife.
She's pulling my slippy
slurpy insides out.
Warm hands.
My tummy feels funny.
Scrape of her spoon
empties and tickles me.

She cut me some eyes.
"Peek-A-Boo! I see you!
So you see me. I'm Dee!"

I'm blinded by brightness,
my inside full of sunshine.
Blue rooster struts by,
cocks his head left
and right to say "Hi."

Dee carves me a nose.
I smell cows in the pasture,
apples in orchards and pies.
Popcorn, candy corn,
caramel in the kitchen.
She sniffs in the cold.
We're nose to nose.

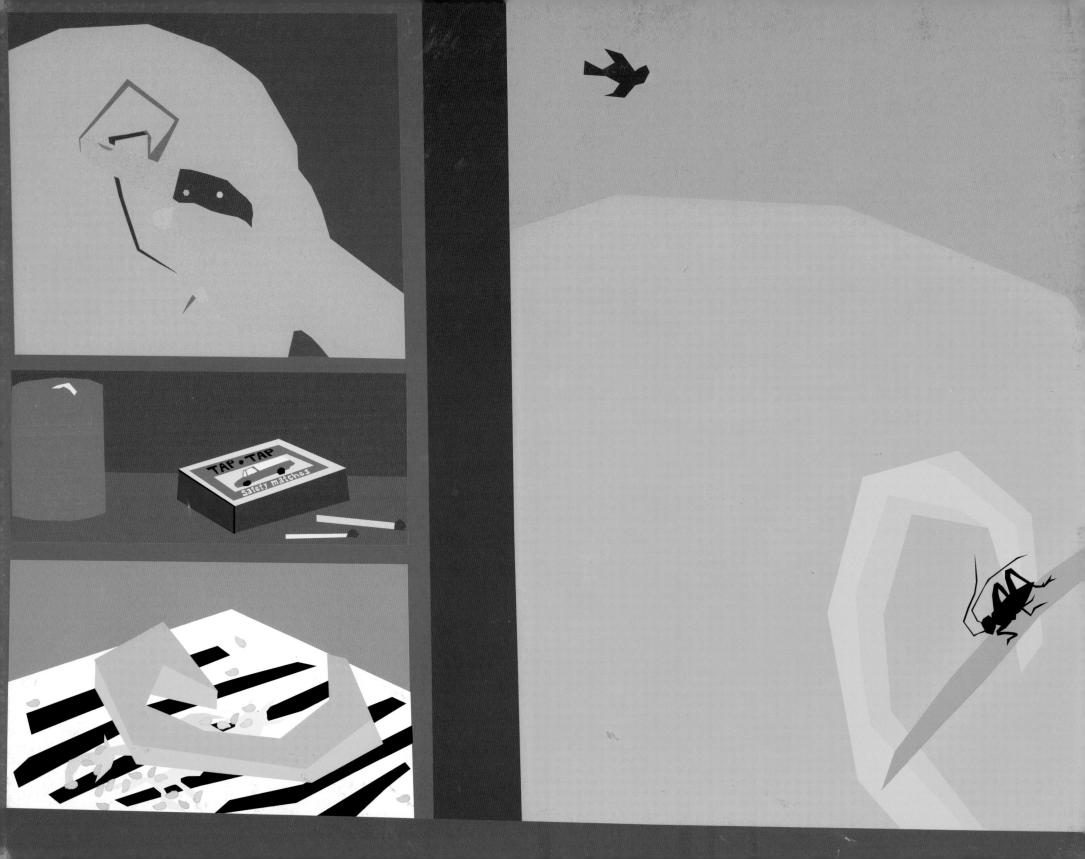

Dee whittles away at my ears and whistles. A horse whinnies, gallops in the pasture.
A cricket sings a small song. Creek runs over stones. A vee of geese honking.
Children joke, giggle and holler.

Dee carves me an ear-to-ear grin. I'm dark inside and Dee lights me. My top fits fine. Three lives I've had, each a surprise that begins the next: silver seed, little pumpkin, jack-o'-lantern. Trick or treat?

At the edge of evening, children
with pumpkins gather in the dusk.
Dee rocks,
hums her pumpkin song,
one she hummed me in the field.
With a candle inside I'm nice and warm.

Orange globes bob in the dark, trick-or-treater mysteries. Dee's friends, and mine from the fields, floating to see me. Tonight we are all someone new.

Laughter, racket, shivaree:
Bang Bang Boom and Rat a Tat Tat

Raucous roister, boisterous noise,
dancing 'til we're breathless and dizzy.

Romping under the pumpkin moon.

At sunrise my candle's gone.
Morning's peace and quiet.
Raccoon nibbles my sooty cooked lid.
Candy and popcorn cleanup crew arrive.

Black Kitty gives me one last shine.
In a week or so my face wrinkles.
My smile's collapsed. I'm feeling sleepy.

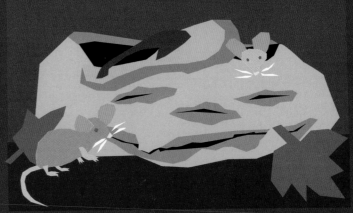

Dee lifts me gently, doesn't mind I'm mooshy. Back across the pasture
to the place I came from. Dee whistles as she walks away.
Left inside of me there's a little silver seed.

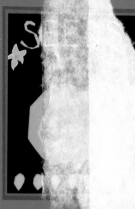